TIMELESS CLASSICS

THE ADVENTURES OF

HUCKLEBERRY FINN

Mark Twain

– ADAPTED BY –

Patricia Hutchison

SADDLEBACK
EDUCATIONAL PUBLISHING

TIMELESS CLASSICS

SADDLEBACK
EDUCATIONAL PUBLISHING
www.sdlback.com

| CONTENTS |

| 1 |

I Join the Robber Gang

I'm Huck Finn. If you read *The Adventures of Tom Sawyer*, you know who I am. That book was made by Mr. Mark Twain. He told the truth, mostly. That book ended when Tom and I got rich. We found some gold in a cave. Some robbers had put it there. We got $6,000 each! Judge Thatcher kept the money for us. We get a dollar a day. That's a lot of money!

Now I live with the Widow Douglas

and her sister, Miss Watson. They are trying to teach me manners. I ran away once, but Tom found me. He said I could be in his robber gang. But only if I went back to the widow's.

The widow read the Bible to me. She meant well. But those stories are about dead people. I didn't care much about them. Miss Watson was worse. "Don't put your feet up there," she'd yell. She'd frown. Sometimes she called me wicked. It made me tired.

I was in my room one night. A spider crawled up my arm. I flicked it off. It landed on a candle and burned up! That was a bad sign. I knew I would have bad luck. Then I heard a noise.

"Me-yow! Me-yow!"

It was Tom. I climbed out the window. Tom and I ran. I tripped and fell. Miss Watson's slave Jim was sitting in the doorway. "Who's there?" he called. We stayed quiet. Then Jim started snoring.

Tom and I went on our way. We met some other boys. We took a boat down the river. Tom showed us a cave in the hill. We crawled in.

"We'll start a gang of robbers," Tom said. "We'll call it Tom's Gang."

Everyone had to swear an oath. No one could tell the gang's secrets. If they did, we would kill their families.

Then someone said, "What about Huck? He doesn't have any family."

I wanted to join them so badly. I *did* have a father. But he was never around. So I said, "I'll give you Miss Watson. You can kill *her* if I talk." They all agreed!

We stuck a pin in our fingers. And we made a mark on a paper with the blood. We wrote our names on the cave wall in blood too. Then we went home.

I climbed in my window. The sun was coming up. My good clothes were dirty. I was dog-tired.

Miss Watson yelled about my clothes. She took me in the closet to pray. One time I tried praying for what I wanted. But it didn't work. What good is a fishing line without hooks?

I hadn't seen my pap for more than a year. That was fine with me. He was always hitting me. I wished he'd never come back.

The gang played robbers for about a month. Then our gang broke up. We hadn't robbed anybody. We just pretended.

One night, I lit the candle in my bedroom. There was Pap. Sitting on the bed waiting for me.

| 2 |

I Fool Pap and Get Away

I was scared to see Pap. He was dirty, and his clothes were rags. His hair was long and stringy. We looked at each other.

He said, "Fine clothes you have there. Aren't you high and mighty?"

"Maybe," I said.

"Don't talk back. I hear you can read and write. You think you're better than

me, don't you?" Pap asked. "Who put you up to that?"

"The widow. She taught me."

"She should mind her own business. You stop that schooling, you hear? Let me hear you read something."

I took a book and began to read. Pap threw it across the room.

"You *can* read. I'll beat you good. Where's that money you have? I came to get it."

"It's a lie! I don't have any money. You can ask Judge Thatcher." That was the truth. I didn't have any money. It was all in the bank.

"I *will* ask him. Got anything in your pocket?"

"Just a dollar," I said. Pap took it. He wanted whiskey.

The next day, Pap went to Judge Thatcher. He tried to get my money.

Judge Thatcher and Widow Douglas went to court. They tried to get me away from Pap. The new judge didn't know Pap. He said he should get another chance.

That judge soon found out about Pap. Pap got drunk. He fell off a porch. Broke his arm sure enough.

But he got better. He chased me when he saw me going to school. I didn't really care about school. I went just to make Pap mad.

Pap waited for me one spring day. He caught me. He took me to an old log hut and locked me up. There was no way for me to get away.

I got used to the lazy life. I sort of liked it. But I didn't like when Pap got drunk. He always went after me.

One time he almost killed me. And once he was gone for three days. I was locked in. That's when I made up my mind to get away.

I found an old saw and hid it. When Pap left, I started sawing a hole in the wall. I took the things I needed. I had a canoe I'd found. I filled it with the supplies.

Then I smashed the door of the cabin.

It looked like robbers did it. I made it look like they took me and threw me in the river.

I paddled the canoe to Jackson's Island. Then I took a nap.

A loud sound woke me up. I sneaked to the shore and hid. I saw Pap and Judge Thatcher on a ferryboat. They were talking about my murder. Then they passed out of sight. I knew no one would be hunting for me.

I went back in the woods. I ran right into a campfire. There lay a man rolled up in a blanket! My heart jumped.

| 3 |
Me and Jim Run Off

The man sat up. It was Miss Watson's Jim!

"Hello, Jim!" I shouted.

Jim stared at me. He was scared. "It's Huck's ghost!" he cried.

I made him understand that I wasn't a ghost. I was glad to see him. I told him how I faked my own killing. He said I was really smart.

"What are you doing here, Jim?" I asked.

He looked scared again. "Huck, I ran off. You won't tell on me, will you?"

"They might call me an Abolitionist. But I won't tell. I swear," I said.

"I had to run, Huck. Miss Watson was going to sell me."

Some birds flew over. Jim said that meant it was going to rain. He told me about all kinds of signs. Counting the things you cook for dinner is bad luck. Shaking a tablecloth after sundown is bad luck. Jim was always talking about bad luck.

Then we got to talking about getting rich. "I'm rich now," Jim said. "I'm free!"

The birds were right. It started to rain. Jim showed me a cave. The thunder rumbled outside.

"It's nice in here," I said. "I wouldn't want to be anywhere else."

It rained for ten or twelve days. The river rose. We paddled around in the canoe. We found a raft and hid it in the woods. One day, we watched a *house* float by. We climbed aboard. We peeked into a window. A man was lying on the floor.

"He's dead," said Jim. He wouldn't

let me look at the body. He took some clothes and other things. We loaded our canoe.

Back on the island, I wanted to talk about the dead man. Jim said it was bad luck. We did find eight dollars in the dead man's coat!

"Hey, Jim," I said. "Remember when I touched that snakeskin the other day? You told me it would bring bad luck. But here's eight dollars. That's not bad luck, Jim!" I said.

"Trouble is coming," Jim said.

The bad luck did come. Jim got bit by a rattlesnake. He was sick for four days.

Days went by. The river went down. I got bored, so I decided to row to town.

Jim said I should dress up like a girl. No one would know me.

I put on some clothes we found in the house. After dark, I paddled to town.

I saw a light burning in an old shack. Then I peeped in the window.

Inside was a woman knitting by candlelight. I didn't know her. Good. She wouldn't know me either. I knocked on the door.

"Come in," the woman said.

So I did.

"What is your name?" she asked.

"Sarah Williams," I said. "I'm very tired. My mother is sick. I've come to get my uncle. He lives at the other end of town."

"Well, you can rest here. My husband will take you to your uncle," the woman said.

She started talking. She was telling about the murder of Huck Finn.

"Some people think his pap did it. Others think a runaway slave named Jim did it. There's a reward out for both of them."

I started to say that Jim didn't kill anyone. But I stopped. I didn't want to give myself away. The woman told me she saw smoke on the island. She thought the slave was hiding there. Her husband was going to find out.

I got uneasy. I couldn't hold still. She looked at me closely. The woman asked me, "What did you say your name was, honey?"

"M-Mary Williams," I said. I tried to be calm.

"All right, now, what is your real name?" she asked. "Bill? Tom?"

I knew it was no use. "It's George Peters. My family sent me to work for a mean man. I ran away. I have to go now."

"Bless you, then. Go. And good luck!" she told me.

I ran out as fast as I could. When I got to the island, Jim was asleep.

"Get up, Jim," I hollered. "We have to go. They're after us!"

| 4 |
The Snakeskin Does Its Work

Jim was scared. We got the raft and loaded it. We tied the canoe behind. Then we shoved off.

At dawn, we tied up and hid in a cove. We lay there all day. Rafts and steamboats floated past.

When night came, we felt safer. Jim built us a tent on the raft. He made a fire. We fixed a stick to hold a light. That way we could warn steamboats not to run us over.

We traveled at night and hid by day. The fifth night, we passed St. Louis. The lights were so bright. It was like the whole world was lit up!

I went ashore each night to get food. Sometimes we shot birds. We lived the good life. It was fun drifting down the river. We would lie on our backs and look up at the stars.

In three more nights, we would be in Cairo. That was Illinois. We would sell the raft. Then we'd take a steamboat. We were headed for the free states. There would be no trouble for Jim there.

The second night, a fog came in. We wanted to tie up. I got in the canoe and paddled ahead. Jim was on the raft. The current picked up. I lost Jim and the raft in the fog. I paddled after them.

I couldn't tell where I was going. There was nothing to do until the fog cleared. I lay down for a nap.

When I woke up, the stars were out. The fog was gone. I looked around. I saw the raft!

Jim was aboard, sound asleep.

I tied up the canoe and climbed aboard. I lay down beside Jim.

"Is that you, Huck? You didn't drown? You're back! Thank goodness."

Then we talked about Cairo. We started worrying that maybe we'd passed it in the fog. If so, we'd be back in slave country again. Jim wanted to get to a free state. He wanted to save money to buy his family from their masters.

Soon, we saw a light.

"That's Cairo!" Jim yelled.

"I'll go see," I said.

"I'll soon be a free man. It's all because of you, Huck. You're my best friend," Jim said.

When I got in the canoe, I felt all mixed up. Maybe it was wrong to help Jim run off. It was sort of like stealing someone's property. I didn't know what to think. Just then, a boat came along. Two men were on board. They had guns.

"We're looking for five slaves that ran off last night," said one man. "I see a man out there on your raft. Is he black or white?"

"He's white."

"We'll go see for ourselves," said the man.

"Wish you would," I said. "It's my pap. He's sick. Everyone's afraid to help him."

"What's wrong with him?"

"It's the … well, it's nothing much."

The man looked scared. "Your pap's got smallpox, doesn't he? Keep away! We won't go near him. Look, here's twenty dollars. I don't want smallpox."

Then the other man gave me twenty dollars too.

I took the money and started back to the raft. I helped Jim get away again! I should have felt bad. But I would feel worse if I turned him in. I decided I wouldn't let it bother me anymore.

I climbed back in the raft. Jim was gone! Then I saw his head sticking out of the water.

"Here I am, Huck! I was going to swim away if those guys came. But you fooled them! You saved Old Jim."

Soon, we saw more lights. I went toward shore.

There was a man on the docks. "Is this town Cairo?" I asked him.

He said no and pointed upriver.

When I told Jim, he didn't say much. We both knew I should not have touched that snakeskin.

A steamboat came pounding up the river. We lit the lantern. We didn't want it to run us over.

We heard bells ringing. Someone was yelling. The steamboat smashed into the raft!

I dove to the bottom. When I came up, I yelled for Jim. But he didn't answer.

| 5 |

The Grangerfords
Take Me In

I swam for shore. I started walking down a road. I came across a big house. Dogs started barking.

"Who's out there?" a man called out a window.

I said, "It's me, George Jackson, sir."

"What do you want?"

"I don't want anything. I was just passing by. I fell off the steamboat. I'm only a boy, sir."

"If you're telling the truth, you don't need to be afraid. Stay where you are. Bob, Tom, fetch your guns and take a look."

I heard people moving in the house. Then I saw a light.

"George Jackson, do you know the Shepherdsons?"

"No, sir. I never heard of them."

"Step forward, George Jackson. Go slow."

I went in the house. There were three men, an old lady, and two young women. They were all staring at me.

The oldest man said, "He's not a Shepherdson."

The old lady saw I was wet. "Buck!" she called.

Buck came down the stairs. He was a boy my age. He took me upstairs and gave me some of his clothes to wear.

The Grangerfords were really nice. They had a nice house too. The door had a brass knob. The table had a fine cloth on it. They ate good food. They must have owned a hundred slaves.

I told them my whole family had died. I said I was going to start a new life. They said I could stay with them as long as I wanted.

I slept in Buck's room. The next morning, I forgot what name I gave myself. I lay there thinking. I asked Buck if he could spell.

He said yes.

"Bet you can't spell my name," I said.

"G-e-o-r-g-e J-a-x-o-n," he said.

"Well, you did it!" I said. I made sure to write it down. I didn't want to forget my name again!

There were a *lot* of Grangerfords. They were fine people. The men were tall. The women were pretty.

Each person had a slave to wait on them. They gave me a slave too. His name was Jack. I wasn't used to having anybody wait on me.

Buck said there used to be more Grangerfords. The Shepherdsons had killed a few. There was a lot of talk about killing. The Grangerford men always carried guns.

The Shepherdsons were another rich family. Buck explained it to me. "Sometimes we kill one of them. Or they kill one of us. Soon, everybody will be killed off. Then there won't be any more fighting."

One day, I wandered down by the river. My slave followed me.

"Master George, come down by the swamp with me. I want you to see something," Jack said.

We came to a piece of dry land. There were lots of trees. Not much to see. When I turned, Jack was gone.

Then I looked in some bushes. Jim was lying on the ground!

Jim said he'd swum to shore behind me. He'd been afraid to call out.

He'd patched up the raft. "We can set out as soon as you want to go," Jim said. Jack had found him and helped.

I went back to the Grangerfords' to sleep. When I woke up the next day, the house was quiet. Buck was gone.

I found Jack. I asked him what was going on.

"Miss Sophia's gone! She ran off with a Shepherdson," he said. "The family left with their guns. There's going to be trouble!"

I went looking for Buck. Soon, I heard gunfire. I climbed up a tree so I could see.

I saw some men. They were shooting at each other. I could hear them shouting, "Kill them. Kill them all!" *Bang. Bang. Bang.*

I stayed in the tree until dark. I climbed down and walked along the riverbank. Buck was lying dead by the edge of the water. I cried a little.

I ran to find Jim. I wanted to get back on the river.

I was glad to get away from the fighting. Jim was glad to get out of the swamp. We both said the raft was the best home we could have. You feel really free on a raft.

| 6 |

The Duke and the King

Two or three lovely days went by. We had the river mostly to ourselves. Sometimes we could hear music coming from another boat floating by. It's a fine thing to live on a raft.

One day, I found a canoe. I paddled up the creek to look for some berries.

All of a sudden, some men came running up the path. I was sure they were looking for Jim or for me.

But then they started yelling for me to save them. They were being chased.

I could hear dogs. I let the men board. We got back to the raft and hid in a cove.

"What got you in trouble?" the old man asked the other.

"I've been selling something that cleans your teeth. Trouble is, it takes the enamel off too. What happened to you?"

"Well," the old man said. "I was running a little meeting. I was telling folks about the evils of drink. They loved me until they found my whiskey jug. They wanted to tar and feather me! I decided to move on."

"Old man," said the younger one. "I think we might team up."

"Good idea," the old man said. "Who are you?"

The young man answered, "I am the Duke of Bridgewater. I used to have a good life. Now I'm living with crooks on a raft."

Jim and I felt sorry for him.

The old man was quiet. Then he piped up. "I am a *king*," he said. "Yes, I am the King of France!"

Jim and I stared. We felt sorry for him too.

After a while, I realized they weren't royalty. They were just liars. But I didn't let on. The best way to get along with people is to pretend to let them have their own way.

They asked why we traveled at night. Then they asked if Jim was a runaway.

"No way," I said. "My pap just died. He left me this raft and his slave. People try to take him. But they leave us alone at night."

The duke had a plan so we could travel during the day. He put a sign on Jim. The sign read runaway slave. Then he got a rope. "We'll say we're taking him in," he said. "We'll tie him up when we see anybody."

I thought it was pretty smart. But Jim wasn't happy.

The duke and the king put on shows in the towns. They weren't very good. Most of the time they sold tickets. Then ran off with the money.

Jim said he didn't want anything to do with those men. He said they were rascals. I agreed, but we were stuck with them. Jim was sitting with his head down. I knew he was thinking about his family. Jim was a good guy.

| 7 |
I Trick the Rascals

One day, the king and I were in a town. We heard a story about a man named Peter Wilks. Wilks had died and left three daughters.

Wilks had brothers who lived far away. They were coming to take care of the daughters.

The king started asking a lot of questions. I could tell he was hatching a plan.

I was right. The king told the duke about Peter Wilks. He said they should pretend to be the brothers.

The king, the duke, and I went back to town. We went to the Wilks's house. The men told the girls they were their uncles. They said I was their servant.

The oldest girl's name was Mary Jane. She was so glad to see us.

She led us to the parlor. There was a coffin in the room. The rascals started crying. I was ashamed of them. It made me sick.

Mary Jane told us her father left the girls $6,000 in cash. She left and came back with the money. The king's eyes lit up! Soon, Mary Jane was handing the money over to him.

Later, when they were alone, I saw the king slap the duke on the back. They were so happy about the easy money they had made.

That night I couldn't sleep. I was letting those sweet girls get robbed. I felt terrible. I decided to try and get their money back.

The next morning, I went into the rascals' room. I searched a bit. The money was under the bed. I took it and hid it in the coffin. I wrote Mary Jane a note. It told where to find the money. I

was all set to slip away. Then everything went wrong.

Two men arrived. They said they were Peter Wilks's brothers. They started fighting with the king and the duke. Other people arrived. They started asking questions. The rascals couldn't answer them. The newcomers were the real brothers. Some folks got angry. They started talking about hanging the rascals. I left as fast as I could.

I got back to the raft. I told Jim, "Let's go! We're finally free of them!"

In two seconds, we were gliding down the river. It was good to be free again. Suddenly I looked out at the water. The king and the duke were paddling a canoe as hard as they could.

They climbed aboard. They were mad.

"Trying to give us the slip, were you?" the king asked.

"No, sir! I knew I couldn't help you.

I didn't want to get hung. I thought you were dead. I'm really sorry."

After a while, the king settled down. But he was still angry about the missing money.

We didn't stop for days. The king and the duke planned more ways to get money. Jim and I felt really uneasy. We thought they were going to rob someone's house.

One day, the king said he was going to town. He said the duke and I were to come get him if he wasn't back by noon.

Noon came and we went into town. We found the king drinking whiskey. He and the duke started to argue. Then the duke started drinking whiskey. I waited until they were drunk. Then I left. I hoped I'd never see them again.

I got back to the raft. I yelled for Jim to shove off. Jim was gone!

I went back to the shore. I called and called. I saw a boy. I asked if he'd seen a stranger. He said he'd seen a man leading a slave. The man had sold the slave at the Phelps's place for $40!

I knew the slave was Jim. The king had sold him. I felt so bad for Jim. Now he was a slave again!

I knew what I had to do. I had to steal

Jim back. I knew it was wrong. But he was my friend. "I don't care if I go to hell!" I said aloud. I set out to steal Jim.

| 8 |

I Have a New Name

I found my way to the Phelps's place. It was a little cotton plantation. I didn't have a plan. I knew I would think of something. I always did.

When I got to the door, a woman came running out. "It's you. At last!" she said. She hugged me. "I'm so glad to see you!" she cried. "We've been looking for you. Give your Aunt Sally a big hug!"

Now I had to find out who she thought *I* was. Before long, she gave it away.

"Children, come here," she yelled. "Come meet your cousin, Tom Sawyer!"

I almost fell to the ground! It was like being born again. I told them all about the Sawyer family. I was happy. Then I heard a steamboat. I said to myself, what if Tom Sawyer is on that boat? What if he gives me away?

I couldn't have that! I told Aunt Sally I had to go back to town.

Sure enough, on the way I saw Tom Sawyer coming along the road. His eyes popped out when he saw me.

"You must be Huck Finn's ghost! Don't hurt me!" Tom cried. "Why did you come back to haunt me?"

"I didn't come back. I've never been gone!"

"You weren't murdered?" he asked.

"No. I just played a trick on Pap. Touch me if you don't believe it."

He touched me. He felt better. He was so glad to see me! He wanted to hear about my adventure.

I told him the whole story. Then I told him why I was at the Phelps's. "I'm trying to steal Jim out of slavery!" I said.

"*What?*" said Tom.

"I know it's wrong," I said. "But you can't tell on me. Okay?"

"I'll help you steal him!" Tom said.

I was so surprised! Tom Sawyer was a good boy. Now he was going to help me steal a slave! We headed back to Aunt Sally's. I would still be Tom Sawyer. Tom would say he was his brother, Sid.

When we got to the house, Aunt Sally hugged and kissed Tom. "What a great surprise!" she said.

That night we acted like we were going to bed. But instead, we went looking for Jim. We looked all over, but we couldn't find him. We needed an adventure, so we headed for town.

Soon, we heard a lot of noise. A bunch of people came toward us. They were carrying torches. They had two guys tied to a rail. It was the king and the duke! They were covered with tar and feathers.

They had been really mean to Jim. But it still made me sick to see them like that. Human beings can be awful cruel to each other!

We asked some people what happened. They said the men cheated folks out of their money. The whole town had gone

after them.

Tom and I headed back home. There was nothing we could do. I knew I hadn't done anything wrong. But I still felt like it was my fault.

After a while, Tom said, "I bet I know where Jim is. I'll bet he's locked in the old hut. I saw a slave taking food there. I saw him unlock the door. Then he locked it when he left. Uncle Silas has the key."

I knew Tom was right! He was so smart!

"Now we need a plan to steal Jim," Tom said.

| 9 |

Trying to Help Jim

"Have you got a plan yet?" Tom asked.

"My plan is this," I said. "First we find out if Jim is in the hut. Then we get my canoe and raft. We steal the key. Set Jim free. We get back on the river. We hide by day and travel by night. That plan will work, won't it?"

"It will work. But it's too simple. What good is a plan if it's too simple?" Tom asked. He wanted another adventure.

We went to the hut. I saw a loose outside board. "We could pull this board off. Then Jim could crawl through," I said.

"We can find a more exciting plan than that," Tom said. "Hey, I know. We'll dig him out!"

We found an old pick. We dug and dug. After two hours, we had a tunnel into the hut.

Jim was there. He was glad to see us!

"Glory be! It's Huck and Master Tom!" he sang out.

Jim was chained to a bed. "If we can

lift the bed, we can slip off the chain," I said.

Tom just shook his head. He was thinking.

After a while, he said, "Well, I guess we don't need to saw his leg off."

"Why would we do that?" I asked.

"I guess we could make him a rope ladder out of sheets. People who escape always need a ladder," Tom said.

"Well, then, let's do it," I said.

The next night, we left the house

again. We took a bag full of stuff. We had candles and sheets and a white shirt.

Tom said this was the most fun he'd had in ages. He didn't want the plan to be too easy. So he wrote a letter to the Phelps family. It said:

"A gang of crooks is going to steal the slave tonight. Signed, An Unknown Friend."

Tom's letter caused a lot of excitement. Fifteen men with guns stood guard.

Luckily, it was a dark night. We slipped out of the tunnel and headed for the fence. Tom's pants got stuck on a splinter. When he pulled loose, he made a noise.

"Who's that?" a man called out. "Answer or I'll shoot!"

We didn't answer. *Bang. Bang. Bang!* Bullets whizzed around us. We ran as fast as we could.

We got to the canoe and hopped in. We headed to the raft. Tom's leg was hurt.

I said, "Well, Jim, you'll never be a slave again!" We were all very happy. Tom was the gladdest of all. He said this was a true adventure. He had a real bullet in his leg!

It was bleeding pretty bad. We tore up the white shirt and bandaged his leg.

"I'm okay," Tom said. "Let's shove off!"

I got to thinking. "You need to see a doctor," I said.

I headed for town in the canoe. Jim would hide in the woods when he saw the doctor coming.

I found the doctor. I told him my brother and I had been out hunting. I said he had shot himself by accident. I asked if he could help us.

"Who are your folks?" the doctor asked.

"The Phelpses," I said.

"Oh," he said. He got his bag. We started out. He said my canoe didn't look strong enough for two people. Then he told me to wait. He took my canoe.

I sat down and waited. The next thing I knew, I was waking up. I looked up. Uncle Silas was coming around the corner.

"Tom Sawyer! Where have you been?"

"Sid and I have been hunting for that slave," I said. "He'll be back in a minute."

"Sid knows his way home," Uncle Silas said. "Let's go." There was nothing I could do. I went with him.

Aunt Sally was glad to see me. We waited for Sid to show up.

"What's taking him so long?" Aunt Sally asked.

"Sid will turn up in the morning," Uncle Silas said. Aunt Sally said she would wait up for him.

I felt bad for Tom. I got up a couple times. I saw Aunt Sally there. She was looking out the window, crying. I felt a little mean. I went back to bed.

It was dawn when I woke up. Aunt Sally was still sitting by the window, sleeping.

| 10 |

Why They Don't Hang Jim

Uncle Silas went looking for Sid. He didn't find him. At breakfast, he and Aunt Sally looked worried.

Then Uncle Silas said, "I almost forgot. Here is a letter from your sister."

I knew that meant trouble. But Aunt Sally dropped the letter. She saw something moving outside the window.

It was Tom Sawyer! Some men were

carrying him. The doctor and Jim were with them. Jim's hands were tied behind him.

Aunt Sally ran outside. I hid the letter, then I ran out too.

Aunt Sally flung herself at Tom. "Oh, he's dead. I just know it," she cried.

Tom turned his head. He muttered something that didn't make sense.

"He's alive!" Aunt Sally said. "Thank God!"

The doctor took Tom into the house. I followed after the men. I wanted to see what they were going to do with Jim.

The men wanted to hang Jim. They swore at him and slapped him. Jim never said anything. He acted like he didn't know me. They took him to the hut. They chained him up.

Later, the doctor came into the hut. "Don't be too hard on him," he said. "When I tried to cut the bullet out, I couldn't do it. I cried out that I needed help. This slave crawled out of the bushes and helped me. He risked his life for this boy.

"Then some men came by. They grabbed the runaway and tied him up. He didn't cause any trouble. He's not so bad. That's what I think."

The men softened up a little. I was thankful to the doctor. He had a good heart. The men promised not to swear at Jim anymore.

The next morning, Aunt Sally and I waited for Tom to wake up. When he did, he said, "Where's the raft? Where's Jim?"

"It's all right," I said. I didn't want to say too much.

But Tom kept on. "Now we're all safe. Did you tell Aunt Sally?"

"Tell me what?" Aunt Sally asked.

"We set the slave free," Tom said.

"Oh dear," Aunt Sally said. "The poor child is feverish again."

"No I'm not," Tom said. "We had a plan." Then he told her the whole story. He told her how much fun we had. I couldn't stop him.

"Well, I've never heard of such a

thing," Aunt Sally said. "If I ever catch you near him again—"

"Didn't Jim get away?" Tom asked.

"No he didn't!" Aunt Sally said. "He's chained in the hut. He'll stay there until he's claimed or sold!"

Tom's eyes flashed. "Turn him loose! He's as free as any man! Miss Watson died two months ago. She set him free in her will!"

"If he was already free, why did you set him free?" Aunt Sally asked.

"I just wanted an—" Then he looked at the door. "It's Aunt Polly!" he said.

The sisters hugged. I hid under the bed.

"Tom, what have you gotten yourself into?" Aunt Polly asked.

"That's not Tom. That's Sid," Aunt Sally said. "Where's Tom?"

"You mean Huck Finn?" Aunt Polly said. "I see him. Come out from under that bed."

So I came out. Tom's Aunt Polly told them who I was. I had to tell the truth. Aunt Sally wasn't mad.

Aunt Polly said that Tom was right about Jim. Miss Watson had set him free. We had gone to all that trouble to free someone who was already free!

"I got a letter saying Sid was here. That's when I knew something was up. Sally, I wrote you two letters asking what was going on. You never wrote back to me."

"I never got any letters. What could have happened to them?" Aunt Sally asked. They were looking at Tom and me.

We saw it was best to say nothing.

| 11 |

Nothing More to Write

When I got Tom alone, I asked him what he had been thinking. Why had we worked so hard to free a man who was already free?

He said he'd planned it from the start. He wanted to head down the river on the raft for some adventures. Then we'd tell Jim that Miss Watson had set him free. We'd celebrate in style. Then we'd take him home on a steamboat. Jim would have been a hero—and so would we!

I figured it all ended up pretty good.

We had Jim out of the chains. Everyone made a big fuss over him. He got lots of food to eat. When he was through, he came up to Tom's room. We had a good talk.

Tom said he wanted the three of us to sneak out. He wanted to go on some more adventures.

I said I didn't have any money for supplies. I figured Pap had gotten all my money from Judge Thatcher.

"No, Huck, the money's still there," Tom said. "Your pap hasn't been back."

Then Jim spoke up. "He's not coming back anymore, Huck."

I asked Jim what he meant.

"Never mind. He's just not coming back, that's all," Jim said.

I kept at him.

At last, Jim said, "Remember the floating house? I said not to look at the dead man. It was your pap."

———— ••• ————

Tom is almost all better. He put the bullet from his leg on a watch chain. He wears it around his neck.

I guess there's nothing more to write about. And I'm glad. It was a lot of trouble to write a book. I'm not going to do it anymore.

I'm going to take the raft out now. I gotta get out of here. Aunt Sally wants to adopt me. She wants to civilize me. I couldn't stand that. I've been there before.